It's a Chi~~ken Pox~~ Epidemic!

Annie and Mr. K. walked Olmo, Georgia, Becca, and Gregory home. When they reached their home, Mrs. K. gave Annie a hug. Then she stared at Annie's face with a worried expression.

"What's the matter, Mom?" asked Annie. "Why are you staring at me?"

"There's a little spot on your forehead," said Mrs. K. "I think you might have chicken pox!"

Other Bantam Skylark Books you will enjoy
Ask your bookseller for books you have missed

Annie K.'s Theater

The Chicken Pox Party

by
Sharon Dennis Wyeth

With illustrations by
Heidi Petach

A BANTAM SKYLARK BOOK®
NEW YORK · TORONTO · LONDON · SYDNEY · AUCKLAND

RL 3, 007–010

THE CHICKEN POX PARTY

A Bantam Skylark Book / December 1990

Skylark Books is a registered trademark of Bantam Books, a division of Bantam Doubleday Dell Publishing Group, Inc. Registered in U.S. Patent and Trademark Office and elsewhere.

Published by arrangement with Parachute Press, Inc.

ISBN 0-553-15839-2

Published simultaneously in the United States and Canada

Bantam Books are published by Bantam Books, a division of Bantam Doubleday Dell Publishing Group, Inc. Its trademark, consisting of the words "Bantam Books" and the portrayal of a rooster, is Registered in U.S. Patent and Trademark Office and in other countries. Marca Registrada. Bantam Books, 666 Fifth Avenue, New York, New York 10103.

PRINTED IN THE UNITED STATES OF AMERICA

OPM   0 9 8 7 6 5 4 3 2 1

For
Sam, Luke, and Avery Fox

Annie K.'s Theater
The Chicken Pox Party

Chapter One

The New Girl

It was a chilly Thursday after school. Annie Kramer and her friends Gregory, Olmo, and Georgia were in their hideout next to Annie's house. The hideout was a grassy circle partly hidden from the road by clumps of trees. Annie and her friends liked to put on plays there. Right now they were working on their next play.

Annie and Olmo were painting red dots on each other's faces. "Perfect," Annie said.

Just then Annie's friend Becca walked into the hideout.

"Where have you been?" Annie asked her. "We've been waiting for you."

"My mother took me shopping after school," said Becca. "I got some new shoes." Becca pointed her toe proudly. "Do you like them?"

Everyone looked at Becca's shoes. They were shiny black patent leather party shoes.

"Ooo," said Georgia. "They're beautiful."

"Aren't you afraid you'll get them dirty?" asked Annie. "They look pretty fancy just for playing."

"I'll be careful," said Becca. "What are you guys all doing?"

"Guess," said Annie.

Becca looked at her friends' spotted faces. "Are you playing connect-the-dots?" she said. "Are you pretending to be clowns? Or are they polka dots?"

Olmo, Gregory, and Georgia giggled, but Annie frowned. "Wrong," she said. "These are chicken pox, not polka dots. I have a great idea for a new play about chicken pox."

"They don't look like chicken pox," said Becca.

"They do, too!" said Annie. Becca was Annie's best friend—but sometimes she had a

2

way of just ruining things, Annie thought.

"Mary Bailey had the chicken pox last week," said Becca. "*Her* spots were brown, not red. And they weren't so round."

"Well, I saw Gordon Grinkov's chicken pox," said Annie. "And his were red."

"I had chicken pox last year," said Olmo. "When I was six. And they looked a lot like this." He pointed to Annie's face.

"I had chicken pox, too!" said Georgia.

"You did not," said Gregory. "You're too little!" Georgia was only four and sometimes she made up things.

"I did too have them. My cousin gave them to me," Georgia insisted. "Have you had them yet?" she asked Gregory.

"No," said Gregory.

"Neither have I," said Becca. Becca was eight, the same age as Gregory, one year older than Olmo and one year younger than Annie.

"Neither have I," said Annie.

"Well, you've got 'em now!" Olmo picked up Gregory's paintbrush and dotted his face with chicken pox paint.

"Hey!" said Gregory.

Annie brushed her bangs out of her eyes

and studied Gregory's face. Then she laughed. "Not bad, Olmo. Those spots look pretty real to me."

"Hey, Annie," said Becca. "When is our chicken pox play going to be?"

"A week from Saturday," said Annie.

"A week from Saturday!" Becca exclaimed. "We'd better get busy!"

"Okay," said Annie. "Here's what happens. There is a chicken pox epidemic. Everyone is sick. Gregory is the doctor, and—"

Just then they heard a dog's bark and a loud screech. *Reeow!*

"What was that?" asked Gregory.

Reeow! There was another screech and more barking.

Annie knew that screech, all right. It belonged to her cat, Bomber!

All five kids raced into Annie's yard in time to see Bomber being chased by a very large dog.

"Bomber!" cried Annie. "Come here!"

Bomber rushed into Annie's arms with the dog at her heels.

Georgia stepped in front of the dog and put out her hand like a crossing guard. "Stop!" she yelled. The big dog screeched to a halt and looked at Georgia obediently.

"Now sit!" said Georgia.

The dog sat down.

Annie rubbed Bomber's ears to calm her down. "Wow," she said to Georgia. "That was amazing."

"Like magic," said Becca.

"Thank you," said Georgia shyly. She began to pet the dog. It had a long, pointed face and very long hair.

Annie noticed a girl standing at the edge of the trees. She was tall and thin, with a long face and very long hair, just like the dog. The girl was watching Annie and her friends. Annie didn't know who she was. But she was going to find out.

With Bomber safely in her arms, Annie walked up to the strange girl. "Hi," she said. "Who are you?"

"I'm Harriet Wise," said the girl. "And that's my dog, Queenie."

"That's *your* dog?" said Annie. "You should keep her in your own yard. She scared my cat to pieces."

"Yeah," said Olmo. "She practically swallowed Bomber in one gulp!"

"I'm very sorry," said Harriet. "Queenie is usually well behaved."

"Well, she was not very well behaved just now," said Annie. She turned away from Harriet and walked back to her friends.

"Here, Queenie," Harriet called. "I'll just take her home now," she said. Then she looked at all the spotted faces around her. "Excuse me," she said. "But do you all have chicken pox?"

Annie grinned at Becca. "See," she said. "They *do* look like chicken pox."

"It's just paint," said Gregory.

"We're doing a play about chicken pox," said Annie.

"A play!" said Harriet. "That sounds like fun. Can I see it?"

"No," said Annie. "It's not ready yet. But you can watch us rehearse if you want to."

"Thank you," said Harriet.

"I'm Annie Kramer," said Annie. "But my friends call me Annie K. And this is Gregory, Becca, Olmo, and Georgia."

"Pleased to meet you," said Harriet.

Harriet and Queenie followed the others back to the hideout. Annie put Bomber down on the grass. Bomber looked at Queenie. Queenie did not seem to notice Bomber anymore. So Bomber sat calmly by a tree.

"Okay, everybody," said Annie. "Here's the new play. There's a chicken pox epidemic. First one kid gets chicken pox. That's you, Georgia. One day you come home from school. You don't feel well. You have a fever."

"Oh, my aching head!" cried Georgia, clutching her forehead.

"Not a headache," said Annie. "A fever."

"Oh, my aching fever!" said Georgia.

"Your mother takes your temperature," Annie went on. "Becca, you can be the mother."

"Okay," said Becca. "I take her temperature. Then what?"

"You call the doctor," said Annie. "That's Gregory. He's the only doctor in the world."

"Who am I?" asked Olmo.

"You are the second kid to get chicken pox," said Annie. She was beginning to get excited now that the play was under way. She went on.

"Soon all the kids in the world have chicken pox. They have to close the schools. And there is only one doctor. He has to work very hard, trying to cure all the children."

"I'm not sure I like this play," said Gregory.

"Me, neither," said Becca.

"Just listen," said Annie. "The doctor gets very tired. The teacher has been helping him, but then *she* gets chicken pox, too." Annie paused. "Wait a second," she said. "We need a teacher."

"Harriet can be the teacher," said Becca.

"Oh," said Harriet. "I'm not sure I can be in the play. I have to ask my mother."

"She won't mind," said Becca. "All our parents come and watch our plays. They like them!"

"I can't do it today," said Harriet. "I'll ask my mother if I can do it another day. Now I have to go home. I promised my mother I'd help her clean out the attic this afternoon."

"Where do you live?" asked Gregory.

"On—" Harriet started to tell them and then stopped. "I have to go," she said quickly. "But I'll come back tomorrow, and maybe I will be the teacher." She stood up and said, "Come on, Queenie."

"Well, okay," said Annie. "See you tomorrow."

"Good-bye, everyone," said Harriet. "It was nice to meet you all."

"Bye," everyone said in unison.

Annie watched Harriet and Queenie go. "Hmmm," she said out loud, "very mysterious."

"What's so mysterious?" asked Gregory.

"Harriet lives in our neighborhood," said Annie, "and I've never seen her before today."

"She probably just moved here," said Gregory.

"But why didn't she tell us that?" Annie wanted to know. Besides having an active imagination, Annie liked a good mystery. Where did Harriet come from in the first place? she thought. Why didn't she say where she lives? And why did she keep saying she has to ask her mother about everything?

"Maybe she's a witch!" blurted out Georgia. Just as Annie was on the lookout for mystery, Georgia thought a lot about scary things.

"Harriet does have a pointy chin!" the four-year-old whispered.

"That doesn't make her a witch," said Becca.

Olmo made his voice sound spooky. "Maybe she's a spy hiding secret documents!"

Annie shook her head. "Harriet wasn't dressed like a spy." But she does have a secret, she decided. And I'm going to find out what it is!

Chapter
Two

Rain, Rain, Go Away!

The next day was warm and sunny. After school, Annie, Becca, Olmo, Gregory, and Georgia met at the hideout. They waited and waited for Harriet. But she didn't show up.

"Where is she?" asked Annie. "She promised to come back today."

"I found out where she lives," Olmo said. "My father told me a new family moved in a few weeks ago. They live in a house down the road from us. I'm sure it's Harriet's. We could walk over there and find out if she's coming."

"Good idea," said Annie. "Maybe she forgot about today." She took Georgia's hand, and they all trooped over to Harriet's house. It was on a road that curved away from Annie's, a few houses past Olmo's. It was a big white house with a front porch and red window boxes. There were very neat small flower beds in the yard, with daffodils just springing up.

The five boys and girls marched up the steps, across the porch, and up to the door. Annie rang the doorbell.

Harriet opened the door and stepped out onto the porch. "Hello," she said. She looked surprised to see them.

"Hi, Harriet," said Annie. She got straight to the point. "Why didn't you come and play like you promised?"

Harriet looked down at her feet. "I'm sorry, Annie. I had to help my mother sort the laundry."

"Can you come out now?" asked Gregory.

"Let me ask my mother," said Harriet. "You all wait here." She went inside and shut the door.

Annie, Becca, Olmo, Gregory, and Georgia settled themselves in chairs on the porch.

"It sure looked like she didn't want us to go inside," said Annie.

"Maybe they have a dead body in there," said Georgia.

"Maybe the house is messy," said Gregory.

"Maybe they're hiding a secret invention!" said Olmo.

Georgia, Gregory, and Olmo were only kidding. But Annie began to wonder. She didn't have to ask *her* mother every time she wanted to do something. And if her friends came to visit her, she always asked them in. So why didn't Harriet?

Soon Harriet came out carrying a big tray with six bowls of vanilla ice cream on it. "I thought you all might like a snack," she said.

"Great!" said Olmo.

Everyone took a bowl and dug in.

"Hey, Harriet," said Annie. "Can we go inside and see your room?"

Harriet blushed. "Not today," she said. "My mother likes to keep the house very neat."

Annie and Becca looked at each other. This is very strange, their look seemed to say. "Oh," Annie said out loud.

Everyone ate their ice cream in silence. Olmo finished his first. He dropped his spoon into his bowl with a clink and said, "That was dee-licious!"

"What should we do now?" asked Georgia.

Harriet stood up and began to gather up the bowls. "I have to go inside now," she said.

"Want to come over to my house later?" asked Gregory. "We could play kickball or something."

"I can't," said Harriet. "I have to finish my homework before dinner."

"Let's go back to the hideout," said Annie.

"Bye, Harriet," said Becca. "Thanks for the ice cream."

"You're welcome," said Harriet.

"Will we see you tomorrow? We have another rehearsal," said Annie.

"Maybe," said Harriet.

And maybe not, thought Annie.

The next day was Saturday. Annie woke up early, ready to go outside and play. But one glance out the window told her that no one would be at the hideout that day. It was pouring rain—the kind of gray rain that lasts all day.

While Annie stared out the window, the

telephone rang. A moment later Mrs. Kramer called, "Annie! It's for you!"

Annie hopped down the stairs and into the kitchen. She took the receiver from her mother. "Hello?" she said.

"Hi, Annie. This is Harriet."

"Hi, Harriet," said Annie.

"I guess there won't be a rehearsal today," said Harriet.

"No," said Annie. "Not unless it stops raining. The play is too big to rehearse inside."

"So what are you going to do today?" asked Harriet.

"I don't know," said Annie. "There's a school project I guess I could work on. I'm supposed to build a papier mâché volcano."

"That's funny," said Harriet. "I had to make a volcano last fall. It's lots of fun. I could come over and help you."

Annie was surprised that Harriet wanted to come over. She also felt very happy. Maybe now she would get closer to solving the mystery about Harriet.

"Okay," said Annie. "That would be great. Come on over after breakfast."

"Aren't you going to ask your mother if it's all right?" asked Harriet.

"Oh, sure," said Annie. "Hold on." She put her hand over the phone and said, "Mom, is it okay if Harriet comes over?"

"Who's Harriet?" asked Mrs. Kramer.

"You'll find out when she gets here," said Annie with a grin.

Mrs. K. smiled. "Well, in that case, tell her to hurry. I'm eager to meet her."

Annie spoke into the telephone again. "It's okay," she said. "My mom can't wait to meet you. So, hurry over."

"Great!" said Harriet. "See you soon."

At ten o'clock a car pulled up to Annie's house.

It was raining so hard that Harriet's father had to drive her over in his car. Annie caught only a glimpse of Mr. Wise, but he didn't look mysterious at all. He just looked like a father. Harriet ran up the front walk in a yellow slicker and matching rain hat.

Mr. K. and Annie let Harriet in.

"Hi, Harriet," said Annie. "This is my father, Mr. Kramer. Dad, this is Harriet."

"Hello, Harriet," said Mr. K. "Let me take your raincoat."

"Hello, Mr. Kramer," said Harriet. "It's nice to meet you." She took off her wet things and handed them to Mr. K.

Bomber jumped onto the couch and put her paw on Harriet's hand.

"She wants you to pet her," Annie said.

Harriet smiled and petted the cat. "My mother won't let Queenie on the furniture," she said.

"Not even on your bed?" Annie asked.

"Never," Harriet said. "Queenie sleeps in the kitchen."

"Oh," said Annie. "Bomber sleeps in my room with me."

Annie led Harriet to the basement. Mrs. K. was there, piling up old newspapers for the girls to use for Annie's volcano.

"Hello, Harriet," said Mrs. K. "It's very nice to meet you. I think everything is all set up here for you girls. Just call if you need any help."

"Thanks, Mom," said Annie. "We will."

Mrs. K. went upstairs. Harriet picked up a sheet of newspaper. "The first thing we have to

do is cut this newspaper into strips. We'll need a whole lot of strips." She picked up a pair of scissors and started cutting. Annie watched her and then did the same.

"Hey, Harriet," said Annie, "how come I never see you at school?"

"What school do you go to?" asked Harriet.

"Middleton Elementary," said Annie.

"I go to Saint Mark's," said Harriet. "That's why you don't see me at school."

"Oh," said Annie. She smiled to herself. No wonder she had never seen Harriet at school. They didn't go to the same school!

"I just moved here a few weeks ago," said Harriet. She kept on cutting paper.

Annie was thinking about the number of times Harriet had to help her mother with housework. "I don't like it when I have a lot of chores," Annie said. "What about you?"

Harriet smiled. "I don't mind."

"Even when you have a lot?" Annie asked.

Harriet just shrugged.

Annie couldn't believe this. "But what about when you want to play, and—"

Annie never finished her question because

just then her mother opened the basement door. "Harriet," called Mrs. K. "Could you come upstairs? Your mother is on the phone."

I'll bet her mother wants her to come home and clean, Annie thought. She didn't want Harriet to leave.

A few minutes later Harriet came back downstairs. She sat down and began cutting paper again.

"Why did your mother call?" Annie asked. She knew she was being nosy, but she couldn't help it.

"She had to tell me something," Harriet answered.

Annie sighed. She had a lot of other questions to ask. She wanted to know what Harriet's mother was like. She wanted to know why her mother was so strict. But how could Annie ask Harriet questions like that?

Harriet interrupted Annie's thoughts. "I like the play you wrote," she said. "The one about the chicken pox."

"Oh, that," said Annie. "The other kids don't like that play. They kept telling me that all the details are wrong. Maybe they are right. Maybe you have to have chicken pox before you can put on a play about it."

"That sounds right," said Harriet.

"Anyway, I'm working on a new play now," said Annie.

"What is it about?" asked Harriet.

"You'll find out soon enough," Annie said mysteriously.

Harriet looked at Annie. "I hope so," she said. Then she put down her scissors. "I think we have enough paper strips now."

Harriet showed Annie how to dip the strips in paste and mold them into a volcano shape. Annie and Harriet decided to make the volcano extra large.

While the papier mâché dried, the two girls went up to the kitchen and ate peanut butter and jelly sandwiches. Soon it was time to paint the volcano.

"Let's paint it purple," Annie said. "With red streaks of lava."

"We can glue little paper trees and houses to its side," said Harriet. "When the volcano erupts all the trees and houses will be covered in lava."

Annie laughed. She was having a great

time. Harriet was wonderful at making vol-canoes. Suddenly Annie knew that she wasn't only interested in solving the mystery about Harriet. She also wanted Harriet to be her friend.

Chapter Three

The Evil Stepmother

The rain finally ended on Monday morning, just in time for school. The sun was warm and strong by the afternoon when Annie, Gregory, and Olmo met at the hideout. Becca soon arrived holding Georgia by the hand, and Harriet came pulling Queenie on a leash. This time, Queenie didn't bark when she saw Bomber. They were beginning to get used to each other and it even looked like they were starting to like each other a little bit.

Annie noticed that Gregory had spots all over his face. She wondered if he had painted them on in preparation for the chicken pox play, the one he didn't like.

"Okay, everyone," said Annie. "Since no one liked the chicken pox play, I came up with a new idea. It's called *The Evil Stepmother.* Here are your scripts."

"Ooo," said Becca. She loved fairy tales. "That sounds good. Can I be the stepmother?"

"No," said Annie. "I'm going to be the step-mother."

"Excuse me," said Harriet. "But if you don't mind, *I'd* really like to be the stepmother."

Annie looked at Harriet in surprise. Then she said. "We can't *all* be the stepmother. Someone has to play the other parts."

"Who will I be?" asked Georgia.

"You will be the princess," said Annie. "Gregory is your father, the king. He is married to the stepmother, and she bosses both of you around all the time. She has you held in captivity. That means you're locked up and can't go out. Olmo is the prince. In the play, he saves you from the stepmother."

"Annie, this play sounds great," said Becca. "*Please* let me be the stepmother! You know

I've always wanted to play an evil queen."

Annie sighed. "All right," she said. "I'll be the director this time." Then she looked at Harriet. "What do you think, Harriet? Will you mind playing a good queen?"

"I really wanted to be the evil stepmother," said Harriet quietly.

"I know," said Annie. "But this is your first play. You can be something evil next time, okay?"

Everyone looked at Harriet. She was staring at her toes. But she said, "Okay."

"Good," said Annie. "Let's start. Everyone is in the castle. Harriet is the good queen. But no one knows she's a queen. Everyone thinks she's a maid."

Becca and Georgia stood in the middle of the hideout. Becca shook her finger at Georgia. "You nasty little insect!" Becca screeched. "I told you to sweep this floor. And look what I found! A speck of dust. You must sweep this floor all over again!"

Georgia got down on her knees. "Oh, Stepmother!" she cried. "I'm too tired to sweep. I've already swept this floor twenty times!"

"Too bad for you!" said Becca. She began to pace back and forth. "I've had just about enough of your laziness. You will be punished!" Becca paused to think for a moment. "But how? I must think of a punishment that is bad enough for a bad girl like you!"

"Please don't punish me!" cried Georgia. "I'll sweep the floor again!"

"Too late!" said Becca. "Tonight you will sleep in the dungeon. With no supper!"

Just then Harriet stepped toward Becca and Georgia. "I have a better idea," she said evilly. "I'll give you some supper, Princess. A supper of frog's eyeballs! Ha ha ha ha ha!"

"Hold it, hold it," said Annie. "What are you doing, Harriet? You're supposed to be *good*!"

"I'm sorry," said Harriet. "I couldn't help it."

"Don't make her be good, Annie," said Olmo. "She was great at being evil! It was fantastic!"

"Becca was evil, too," said Gregory.

"I don't care what you say, Annie," said Becca. "I won't be the good queen!"

Annie folded her arms. Then she unfolded them. Then she folded them again.

"Okay," she said. "We'll have *two* evil step-mothers."

"Hooray!" said Harriet.

"Now, everyone be quiet!" said Annie. "I think you were saying something about frog's eyeballs, right, Harriet?"

"That's right," said Harriet with a cackle. She was being the evil stepmother again. Her pointy face looked pointier than ever. "Frog's eyeballs for supper are worse than no supper at all!"

Georgia pouted and stamped her foot. "I won't eat them!" she shouted. "And you can't make me!"

"Oh, yes we can," said Becca. "We can tickle you with a feather until you can't stand it any longer. *Then* you'll be ready to eat a frog's eyeball."

"I know something even *worse*," said Harriet. "We can lock you in a room full of worms. We won't let you out until you eat at least one frog's eyeball. Won't you have just one teensy, weensy little taste?" She pretended to hold a frog's eyeball up to Georgia's mouth.

Annie said, "Gregory, I think it's time for the king to come in."

Gregory stood up straight. "What are you doing to my daughter?" he yelled. "Leave her alone!"

"Go away, King," said Becca.

"Yes," said Harriet. "Go wash the dishes. Or else we will put *you* in a room full of worms!"

"How dare you speak to me like that?" said Gregory. "I am the king!"

"Not for long," said Harriet. "As soon as I get the princess out of the way, I am going to take over the throne!" She turned back to Georgia. "Tell me quick," she said. "The worms or the eyeballs. Choose now or I shall choose for you!"

Georgia started to cry. Olmo stood up and ran into the center of the circle. "Leave her alone," he shouted to Harriet. "You're too mean!"

"Stop it, everyone!" said Annie. "Georgia, what's the matter?"

Georgia sniffed and said, "Harriet is being too scary."

"I'm sorry, Georgia," said Harriet. "I didn't mean to scare you. I was just trying to be a good evil stepmother."

"You *were* pretty scary," said Annie. "Maybe you should try to be a little less evil."

"I'll try," said Harriet.

Just then everyone heard a voice calling, "Harriet!" Then a woman appeared at the edge of the hideout. She had brown hair and a bright red coat.

"There you are, Harriet," said the woman. "I just came to pick you up. Did you forget about that little promise you made this morning?"

"Sorry, Mom," said Harriet. "Everyone, this is my mother. Mom, this is Annie, Olmo, Georgia, Becca, and Gregory."

So that's Harriet's mother, thought Annie.

Mrs. Wise said hello to each child. When she saw Gregory her face fell. "What are you doing out of your house?" she snapped.

"Me?" Gregory asked.

"Yes, you!"

"I'm rehearsing," said Gregory.

"Well, you shouldn't be," Mrs. Wise said. "You shouldn't be near other children!"

Gregory looked as if he was going to cry.

Mrs. Wise grabbed him by the hand.

"You've got chicken pox!" she said. "I'm going to take you home now. Do you live nearby?"

Gregory nodded.

"Come on, Harriet," said Mrs. Wise. "We're taking Gregory home. But don't get too close to him, whatever you do!"

"Good-bye, everybody!" called Harriet. She and Queenie and Gregory left with Mrs. Wise.

Everyone sat quietly for a minute. So much had happened in such a short time. No one knew what to say.

Georgia broke the silence at last. "Boy," she said. "Harriet's mother is mean!"

"Did you see the way she just grabbed Gregory and dragged him home?" said Olmo.

"It's scary," said Becca.

"Yeah," said Annie. "It sure is."

Annie's Big Imagination

Mrs. Wise was right. Gregory *did* have the chicken pox. He couldn't go out to play for a while. But he could talk to his friends from his bedroom window.

Annie wanted to keep rehearsing *The Evil Stepmothers,* with or without Gregory. "We can do the scenes that Gregory isn't in," she said.

But Gregory was not the only one who was not at rehearsal. Harriet did not show up the next day. At first, Annie thought Harriet must have been busy with something. But a few days passed, and Harriet still did not show up.

"I wonder where she is?" Gregory called

from his window. The others had gone to his yard to visit him.

"Maybe her mother doesn't like us," said Becca. "She was pretty mean to you, Gregory."

"And she told Harriet to stay away from him," said Georgia.

"Maybe she wants to keep Harriet away from *all* of us," said Annie. She looked at Olmo. He had not said anything yet. But he was smiling a funny, secret smile.

"What are you smiling at?" asked Annie.

Olmo was taking his time answering. This was big news. "I found something out," he said at last.

"What is it?" asked Becca.

"Well," said Olmo, "Harriet's mother is not her mother."

"What do you mean?" asked Annie. "Harriet called her 'Mom.'"

"I know," said Olmo. "But Mrs. Wise is not Harriet's *mother*." He paused.

"Don't just stand there," said Annie impatiently. "Tell us!"

"She's her *step*mother," said Olmo.

"Her stepmother!" said Becca. "How do you know?"

"My mother told me," said Olmo.

"Wait a minute," said Annie. "It's all starting to make sense now."

"What is?" asked Becca.

"The evil stepmother!" Annie whispered. "In real life Harriet is not evil at all. But she knows how to *act* evil!"

"*Really* evil," said Georgia with a shiver.

"So maybe her stepmother is evil to her!" Annie went on. "Remember how we weren't allowed in the house?"

"Yeah," said Olmo. "And she's always making Harriet do chores."

"And she doesn't let Harriet go out very much," said Becca.

"Louder!" called Gregory. He was still leaning out of his window. "What are you guys talking about down there? I can't hear a word you're saying!"

Everyone looked up at Gregory.

"I'm sorry, Gregory," called Annie. "But this is too big a secret to yell. We'll tell you later."

"Later?" said Gregory. "That's not fair. I want to hear about it now. At least tell me what you're talking about."

"We're talking about Harriet!" shouted Georgia.

"Shh!" said Annie and Becca.

Just then Gregory's mother appeared in the window. "Gregory," she said, "that's enough shouting for one day. Come in and rest awhile."

"I have to go in now," Gregory called to his friends. "Don't forget to call me and tell me what you're saying about you-know-who."

"We won't forget!" called Olmo. He waved to Gregory and then turned back to Annie. "What were we saying?" he asked. "I can't remember."

"That we haven't seen her for a week!" said Annie. "Do you know what I think?"

"What?" said Olmo, Georgia, and Becca.

"I think Harriet's stepmother has Harriet in captivity!" said Annie.

"She's probably making Harriet work her fingers to the bone!" said Becca.

"Poor, poor Harriet," said Georgia. "What can we do?"

"I know exactly what we'll do," said Annie. "We'll rescue her!"

"But how?" asked Becca.

"I don't know yet," said Annie. "But I'll think of something."

Later in the afternoon, Annie called Gregory on the telephone. She wanted to fill him in on Harriet. She told him all about Harriet's stepmother keeping her in captivity. "I think we should rescue her," she finished.

Gregory had his doubts about Annie's story. "What if we're wrong?" he asked. "Maybe there is some other reason why Harriet doesn't come to rehearse anymore."

"Maybe," said Annie. "But I know how we can find out for sure!"

"How?" asked Gregory.

"Instead of a rescue mission, we'll go on a *spy* mission," said Annie. "We'll find out if Harriet needs to be rescued. Then we will rescue her if we have to!"

"A spy mission," said Gregory thoughtfully. "We can use my spyglass."

"Perfect!" said Annie.

Just then Mrs. Denton, Gregory's mother, walked into the kitchen and past where Gregory was sitting.

"I've got to get off the phone now," he whispered. "This house is filled with the enemy. From now on we must communicate by secret notes. Go outside to my yard. I will send you a note from my window. Over and out."

"Roger, Gregory," said Annie. "Over and out."

Annie put on her coat and went outside. She crossed her yard and stood in front of Gregory's window. Gregory opened the window and tossed out a paper airplane. Annie ran to catch it. Then she opened it and read it.

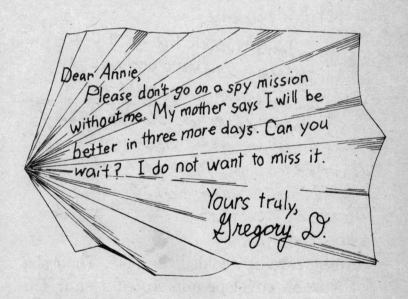

Annie was about to shout her reply to Gregory when he put his finger on his lips. Mrs. Denton's face appeared in the window. "What is this window doing open again, Gregory?" she said. "It's chilly out today." Then she shut the window with a *thwat*!

Annie went back to her own house and wrote Gregory a note.

Dear Gregory,
Don't worry. We won't do the spy mission without you. Besides, we may need your help. Also we don't have a plan yet. Get well soon.
Your friend,
Annie K.

Annie carefully folded the note. Then she put it in an envelope and sealed it shut. On the front of the envelope she wrote: GREGORY D. TOP SECRET. She left the note in Gregory's mailbox.

Top Secret Spy Mission

A few days later Gregory felt much better. There were only two or three spots left on his face. His mother and father told him that he could go outside to play at last. The first thing he did was go to the hideout. Annie, Becca, Olmo, and Georgia were waiting there for him. Everyone was very happy to see him.

"Hurray for Gregory!" said Olmo. "It's good to have you around again."

"Thanks," said Gregory. "Has Harriet been around?"

"No," said Annie. "We still haven't seen or

heard from her. I called her on the phone. But no one answered."

"I can't wait to know what happened to her," said Becca.

"Well," said Gregory, "I'm all ready to find out. I brought my spyglass with me." He pulled the spyglass out of his pocket. It was all folded up.

"Cool!" said Olmo. "This is just what we need."

"Then let's go!" said Georgia.

"Wait a minute," said Annie. "We can't go now, during the day. Someone will see us."

"That's right," said Becca. "We should do our spying at night!"

"No fair!" said Georgia. "I can't go out at night. And I want to go spying, too."

"Don't worry, Georgia," said Annie. "We won't go at night. We'll go just before dinner. I'll ask your mother if you can play a little later today."

"Okay," said Georgia.

So it was settled. Annie called Georgia's mother, who said Georgia should be home by dinnertime. While they were waiting, the kids tried to play kickball in Gregory's yard, but the ground was too wet from the rain. Then they went inside Gregory's house to play in the basement. But no one felt like playing games. They were too excited about their top secret mission to bother with kid stuff.

At last the sun began to go down. Annie, Becca, Gregory, Olmo, and Georgia put on their warm sweaters. Gregory picked up his spyglass, and out they went into the chilly evening air.

The five friends talked as they walked down the road. But they grew very quiet when they saw Harriet's house. No one else was around. The light was growing dim. It was hard to see anything.

Several lights were on in Harriet's house. Annie looked at all the windows, trying to guess which room was Harriet's. She had never been inside the house, so she didn't know where Harriet might be.

Gregory opened his spyglass and peered at the house.

"Can you see anything?" asked Olmo in a whisper.

"No," said Gregory. "We're too far away. We'll have to get closer."

Georgia grabbed Becca's hand. The friends began to tiptoe across the lawn toward the house. The wet ground squished a little under their sneakers.

"What if someone sees us?" asked Georgia.

"Then we'll run!" said Olmo.

"Shh!" said Gregory.

Lights glowed from the first-floor window, next to the porch where they had eaten ice cream. A second-floor light was on, as well as one in the basement.

"The basement!" said Becca. "Maybe Mrs. Wise uses it as a dungeon!"

"Good thinking, Becca," said Annie. "Let's look there first."

Quiet as mice, they crept up to the basement window. It was the easiest window for them to peek through, because it was so low to the ground. Annie got down on her hands and knees and looked inside. She could see a laundry room with a clothes washer and a dryer. Mrs. Wise was pulling clothes from the dryer. Harriet was there, too. She was wearing a bathrobe and sitting on a stool near her stepmother. Neither of them looked very happy.

"Here they are!" Annie motioned to her friends to come closer and look.

Everyone knelt down to peek. Gregory tried to use his spyglass, but he didn't need it. The window was open a crack, and they could see and hear everything pretty well.

Harriet was talking. "Please, Mom," she was saying. "Please let me go out. I'm so tired of being cooped up in here!"

Mrs. Wise turned away from the dryer to speak to Harriet. "Harriet, we have been over this before. The answer is no. I'm sorry, but you know that's how it has to be."

Annie and Becca looked at each other and gasped.

Harriet started crying. "Mom!" she cried. "*Please*. I can't stand being inside anymore!"

Just then headlights flashed across the yard. A car was pulling into the Wises' driveway!

"Someone's coming!" whispered Annie. "Run!"

All five kids darted across the yard to the nearest hedge. They all crouched behind the hedge, peeking at the house.

A man got out of the car and walked into the house.

"That's Harriet's father," whispered Annie.

"Maybe he will help her," said Becca. "I think Harriet is in trouble!"

"Let's get out of here!" said Olmo. They all ran down the road. Once they got around the curve they slowed down and began to walk. They were almost at Gregory's house. Gregory's mother would wonder what they had been doing if they were all out of breath. And they didn't want her to ask them where they had been.

Olmo went home after they dropped off Georgia. Annie, Becca, and Gregory walked the rest of the way together.

"It looks like Mrs. Wise really *does* have Harriet in captivity," said Annie. "We've got to do something!"

"Did you hear what they were saying?" said Becca.

"Harriet said, 'Please let me go! I can't stand it anymore!' And her stepmother said no."

They were back on their street now. Becca's

47

mother stood on the front porch of her house. "Dinner's almost ready!" she called.

"Bye," said Becca. "What do we do next?"

"We'll meet at the hideout after school tomorrow," said Annie. "We're going to save our friend!"

Chapter
Six

The Chicken Pox Picnic

On Tuesday, school seemed to drag on for-
ever. Annie couldn't get Harriet out of her
mind. She fidgeted and squirmed and stared
out the window. I'm glad it's not raining, she
thought, looking at the cloudy sky. Rain would
ruin their rescue mission.

The school day ended at last. Annie got on
the bus and sat in the back. Becca got on a few
minutes later and sat with her. They whispered all the way to their stop. Then they got
off the bus and ran home.

Annie threw her books on her desk and
started back out the door. "I'm going right to

the hideout, Mom!" she called.

Mrs. Kramer appeared from her bedroom. "What's the rush?" she asked. Then she said, "I'll bet I know. It's that play you're doing next Saturday, right?"

The play! Annie had almost forgotten about it. Rescuing Harriet seemed much more important.

The rescue mission was one thing Annie couldn't tell her mother about. But she wasn't going to lie. So she didn't say anything except "Can I please go now?"

"Wait a minute, dear. Are you warm enough in that jacket?"

"I'm warm enough," said Annie. "*Now* can I go?"

"Yes, sweetie," said Mrs. K. "Be back for supper. Your father is making spaghetti and meatballs."

"Okay," said Annie, and she raced out the door to the hideout.

Everyone else was there, ready and waiting.

"Becca," said Annie, "did you tell them our plan yet?"

"No," said Becca. "I was waiting for you."

"I'm glad we have a plan," said Olmo.

"Because the more I think about our rescue mission, the more nervous I get."

"Not me," said Georgia. "I can't wait to save Harriet."

"What's the plan?" asked Gregory.

"It's very simple," said Annie. "We'll look through the basement window to make sure Harriet is alone. Then we'll knock on the window to get her attention. We'll tell her to stand on the stool, open the window, and climb out. It's so easy I can't imagine how we'd fail."

Gregory frowned. "Do you really think it will be that easy?"

"Of course," said Georgia.

"Let's go," said Olmo.

"Ready, everyone?" asked Annie.

"Ready!" said the others, and off they trooped to Harriet's house.

It was almost dark when they reached Harriet's house. Annie, Becca, Gregory, Olmo, and Georgia stopped at the hedge and crouched down to scout the house. Windows were lit on the first and second floors. But the basement was dark.

"Poor Harriet," said Georgia. "Her stepmother keeps her locked in a dark basement!"

Gregory looked around to make sure no one was coming. "The coast is clear," he said, just like in the spy movies. "Let's go."

Everyone ran to the basement window. Olmo put his face up to it and peered in.

"I can't see a thing!" he said.

"Tap on the window," said Becca. "Maybe Harriet will hear us."

Olmo tapped on the window, but no one answered. He put his mouth up to the opening and whispered, "Harriet! Are you in there?" They heard no sound at all.

"Maybe they let her go upstairs and watch TV for a while," said Gregory.

Annie glanced up at the front porch. "We could peek in there," she whispered, pointing to the window next to the porch.

"You mean, go up on the porch?" said Becca. "What if someone catches us?"

"I don't care," said Annie. "I'm so worried about Harriet that it's worth the risk if we can save her!"

Becca, Gregory, and Olmo looked at Annie doubtfully. Georgia said, "*I'll* go with you, Annie."

"Thanks, Georgia," said Annie. "Anyone else want to join us?"

"I will," said Gregory.

"Me, too," said Olmo.

"Well, if everyone else is going, I'll go, too," said Becca.

One at a time they climbed the creaky steps to the porch and crouched beneath the window. Then Annie slowly lifted her head and peered inside. Mrs. Wise was sitting in a chair, watching the news on TV. She was alone in the room.

Georgia tugged on Annie's sleeve. "What's happening up there?" she whispered.

"I'm looking into the living room," Annie whispered back. "Her mother's watching TV. Harriet isn't there."

"Let me see, too," said Olmo. He raised his head to look through the window.

"If Olmo gets to look, I want to look, too," said Georgia. She stood up next to Annie. Then Gregory and Becca stood up, too.

Mrs. Wise must have felt all those eyes staring at her, for just at that moment she turned her head toward the window. Then she screamed!

"Oh, no!" said Annie. "Let's get out of here!"

The five kids hurried off the porch at top speed, but Georgia, who couldn't run as fast, was left behind. Mrs. Wise rushed out the front door and grabbed her by the seat of her pants.

"Annie! Annie!" cried Olmo. "She's got Georgia!"

Annie and the other kids stopped running and turned to face the house. Scared as they were, they couldn't leave without Georgia. Her mother would be so angry!

"What's going on here?" demanded Mrs. Wise. "Who's out there?"

Annie gulped. "It's only us, Mrs. Wise," she said. "Harriet's friends."

Mrs. Wise moved closer and peered into the darkness. "Now I recognize you," she said. Her voice was softening a little. "You're Annie, and Becca, and Olmo. And Gregory, the one with the chicken pox. How are you feeling, Gregory?"

"Much better, thank you," said Gregory.

"We came to see Harriet," said Becca.

"How sweet!" said Mrs. Wise. "Come in, come in! She will be so happy to see you. She's

54

been so bored ever since she came down with the chicken pox."

"The chicken pox!" said Annie. "Is that why she hasn't come out to play?"

"Didn't you know?" said Mrs. Wise. "She's begun to feel better, and has been begging me to let her go outside to join you all. But the doctor told me not to let her out until Saturday. Oh, it's so nice of you kids to come and visit her." She opened the door to let Harriet's friends inside. "Wipe your feet on the mat, please," she added.

Annie looked down. Their shoes *were* a bit muddy.

"Gosh," Becca whispered in Annie's ear. "She isn't acting like an evil stepmother."

Annie's cheeks turned red as she wiped her feet. It looked as if she had been all wrong about Mrs. Wise.

Then Georgia stopped in the doorway. "I'm not going in there!" she said, pointing to Mrs. Wise. "She's evil!"

"What?" said Mrs. Wise. "What are you talking about?"

Annie rushed to Georgia's side. "Shh," she told her. "Mrs. Wise isn't evil."

"But *you* said she was!" insisted Georgia.

Annie's face reddened even more. She knew Georgia was right.

"I know that, Georgia. But I guess I was wrong," Annie said. It was difficult for Annie to admit she was wrong sometimes. She turned to Mrs. Wise and said, "I'm sorry."

"I understand," said Mrs. Wise. She was smiling. "Go on upstairs, kids. Harriet's room is on the left."

Annie, Becca, Gregory, Olmo, and Georgia trooped upstairs and into Harriet's room. Harriet was sitting up in bed, reading a storybook. She had more spots on her face than Gregory did. But she looked pretty well. Queenie sat next to her bed.

"Harriet!" cried Georgia. "You're all right!"

"Hi!" said Harriet. "I'm so glad you guys came. I've missed you!"

"We missed you, too," said Annie. "We were worried about you."

"You were?" said Harriet.

"Of course we were," said Gregory. "We didn't know you had the chicken pox."

"Did you do the play without me?" asked Harriet.

"No!" said Annie firmly. "How could we do the play without you? You're so good at being evil."

Harriet blushed and looked very happy.

"When will you be all well?" asked Olmo.

"In a couple of days," said Harriet. "I'm not contagious anymore, so don't worry. I can't wait to go outside. I've been so bored just sitting here with no one but Queenie. I wish I could go outside now!"

"You can't go out just yet, Harriet," said Mrs. Wise. She was standing in the doorway. "But maybe your friends would like to stay for dinner. We have plenty of pizza. We could spread a blanket on the floor in here and make it a picnic. What do you say?"

"Yes!" cried all the kids.

"A chicken pox picnic!" said Annie.

Mrs. Wise laughed. "I'll call everyone's parents to make sure it's okay." Then she kissed Harriet on the top of her head and left the room.

Mrs. Wise really loved Harriet, Annie thought. She knew she would never tell Harriet that they had all thought her stepmother was evil. She wouldn't even say that she knew Mrs. Wise was her stepmother. Instead, she said, "Your mother is really nice, Harriet."

"I know. I was so happy when she and my dad got married. You know, she's my stepmother."

"She is?" said Annie, pretending to be surprised.

"Yes," said Harriet. "My real mother died when I was very young. Now I've got a real family again."

"Don't forget your friends," said Olmo.

"And you're all good friends," Harriet agreed.

"This is getting too mushy," Gregory said. He looked at Queenie. "Can your dog do tricks?" he asked.

"A few," Harriet told him.

Everyone watched as Harriet had Queenie shake her paw and roll over. She even stood on her hind legs.

Mrs. Wise came in to say that all of the mothers said yes to the chicken pox picnic. Before long, two large pizzas arrived. Everyone settled down on the floor. "This is just like an outdoor picnic," said Olmo. "Without the ants," he added.

Everyone talked and laughed and enjoyed their pizza. Gregory and Harriet compared chicken pox stories.

"I have an announcement to make," Annie said. "Since Gregory is well and Harriet is almost well, we can rehearse *The Evil Step-mothers* again. The new performance day is a week from Saturday. Is that okay with you all?"

"Yes!" everyone said.

"Good," said Annie.

Annie's father came to pick up the kids after supper. "Thank you for our chicken pox party," said Annie.

"You're welcome," said Mrs. Wise. "I hope you'll all come back and visit again soon."

"She seems like a very nice woman," said Mr. Kramer as they strolled down the street.

"She is," said Annie. It was hard to believe she had ever thought Mrs. Wise was evil.

Annie and Mr. K. walked Olmo, Georgia, Becca, and Gregory home. When they reached their home, Mrs. K. gave Annie a hug. Then she stared at Annie's face with a worried expression.

"What's the matter, Mom?" asked Annie. "Why are you staring at me?"

"There's a little spot on your forehead," said Mrs. K. "I think you might have chicken pox!"

"Oh, no!" said Annie.

Mrs. K. called the doctor and sent Annie straight to bed.

The next day Annie didn't go to school. After lunch, she was so lonely, she decided to call Harriet.

"Hi, Harriet," said Annie. "Guess what?"

"What?" said Harriet.

"I've got the chicken pox!"

"You, too?" said Harriet.

The two girls laughed.

"This is just like your chicken pox play," said Harriet. "It's a chicken pox epidemic! And it means we will have to postpone *The Evil Stepmothers*—again!"

"Come to think of it," said Annie, "I *still* want to do a play about the chicken pox. But it will be different this time. It will be about our chicken pox party!"

"Remember what you told me last week,"

said Harriet. "You said that maybe you have to have the chicken pox before you can make a play about it. That means *The Chicken Pox Party* will be your best play yet!"

Annie K.'s Play

THE CHICKEN POX PARTY

Time: The present
Place: A make-believe village in a made-up kingdom

Characters

THE STORYTELLER
WERU—a boy who is very good at contests
WERU'S FRIENDS—the other children in the village
THE SORCERER
THE KING
THE QUEEN

Props

A headdress with feathers
A hula hoop
A rope
A broomstick
A crown
A bag of peanuts
A cardboard box big enough for Weru to sit down in (the chicken pen)
Three feathers
A second bag of peanuts

A bag of candy corn (the chicken feed)
A bag of a different kind of candy

(The Storyteller is seated on the ground. All the children in the play are seated around him.)

STORYTELLER
I will tell you a story!

CHILDREN
Hooray!

STORYTELLER
Everyone will act out the parts. It is the story of a boy named Weru.

ONE CHILD
(Standing up) I will be Weru.

STORYTELLER
Good. (Pointing to the other children) And you will be the king. You will be the queen. You will be the sorcerer. And the rest of you will be Weru's friends.

WERU

We are all ready.

STORYTELLER

Once upon a time there was a very strong child named Weru. Weru lived all alone with no parents. The queen in the village wanted to adopt Weru.

QUEEN

I have no children, Weru. Will you be my child?

WERU

No. I can take care of myself.

STORYTELLER

Weru was very good at games. He and his friends played in the village.

(Weru and his friends play a game of tug-of-war with a rope; Weru holds one end of the rope. The other children all hold the other end. Weru wins the game.)

FRIENDS

You have won, Weru!

(The King and Queen hold a broomstick and the children try to dance under it. When the broomstick is very low, only Weru can manage to dance under it.)

KING AND QUEEN

Look at Weru! He is wonderful!

QUEEN

Weru is such a wonderful child. If only I could have him for my son.

KING

Weru wants to take care of himself.

STORYTELLER

Of all the games he liked to play, Weru liked playing with the hula hoop best.

(Weru picks up the hula hoop and jumps through it; he then twirls it around his waist.)

KING

Weru is very good at the hula hoop.

QUEEN

All of the children like the hula hoop. Let's have a hula hoop contest!

KING

The winner will wear a crown. (He shows the children the crown.) I will also give the winner a big bag of peanuts. (He shows the children the big bag of peanuts.)

STORYTELLER

All of the children were excited. They practiced with their hula hoops. (Weru and his friends take turns practicing with hula hoops or each practice with one of their own.)

WERU

No one is better than I am at the hula hoop! I am sure to win the contest.

STORYTELLER

Weru and his friends went home and went to sleep. The next morning was the day of the contest. Weru woke up and there were red marks on his face!

WERU

(Touching his face) Oh, no! What is wrong with me?

QUEEN

My goodness! You have the chicken pox!

KING

Go home, Weru. You cannot be in the hula hoop contest.

STORYTELLER

Weru left. He was very angry. He went to see the sorcerer.

WERU

I want to be in the contest. You must cure me!

SORCERER

The only cure for the chicken pox takes ten days.

WERU

I cannot wait ten days. I want to win the contest! Can't you do something? Do anything! Put a spell on me to get rid of these marks.

SORCERER

(Handing him the feather headdress) Here is a disguise. Put it on, and you will look like a chicken. No one will know that you are Weru, and that you have the chicken pox.

STORYTELLER

Weru put on the disguise and went to the contest.

WERU'S FRIENDS

Look! A chicken! A chicken wants to be in the contest!

QUEEN

Poor Weru. Too bad he has the chicken pox. He is very good at hula hoops.

KING

Let the chicken be in the contest instead.

STORYTELLER

Underneath his disguise, Weru was very happy. He had fooled the king and queen and all his friends.

WERU

No one knows who I am. They think I am a chicken, but I am really Weru.

STORYTELLER

The contest began. Weru's friends and the chicken each took a turn at the hula hoop.

KING

The chicken is best! The chicken is the winner.

QUEEN

(Bringing the crown) Here is the crown. (She tries to put the crown on over Weru's disguise, but it won't fit.) The crown won't fit, but you may keep it, chicken.

KING

And here is your prize. A big bag of peanuts.

(Weru takes the crown and bag of peanuts and starts to walk away.)

QUEEN

Wait! That chicken is very unusual. I think we should keep him.

KING

Very well. Catch the chicken, children.

STORYTELLER

The children caught the chicken and put him in the pen.

(Weru's friends catch him and make him step into the chicken pen. They put his crown and bag of peanuts in with him.)

KING

He is now the royal chicken.

QUEEN

He is my pet.

KING

(Giving the children a bag of chicken feed) It is your job to feed this royal chicken, children.

STORYTELLER

Weru sat in the pen while his friends threw corn at him.

WERU'S FRIENDS

(Tossing food into the pen) Here, royal chicken. Have some corn.

STORYTELLER

His friends saw the bag of peanuts inside the pen and wanted it.

FRIENDS

Give us that prize! Chickens do not eat peanuts.

STORYTELLER

But Weru wanted to keep the prize for himself.

WERU

(Holding the bag of peanuts) No, go away! It is mine.

STORYTELLER

Weru's friends went away to play. Weru felt lonely. Soon the queen came to visit him.

QUEEN

Poor chicken, you look very lonely. I am lonely, too, for a child. But now I have you to keep me company.

STORYTELLER

The queen petted Weru and took care of him. Weru liked it. But the king called the queen away.

KING

Come here. You are spending all your time with your new pet. That is not a child, remember. It is a chicken.

STORYTELLER

When the queen left, Weru was lonely again. He wanted to get out of the pen. He tried to take off his disguise, but he couldn't.

WERU
The chicken disguise is stuck. What am I going to do?

STORYTELLER
He called to his friends.

WERU
Friends, come and rescue me. I am not a chicken. I am Weru.

STORYTELLER
But his friends were too busy playing games to hear him.

(Weru's friends play tug-of-war and then play with their hula hoops.)

STORYTELLER
Days went by and Weru's friends began to wonder how he was. They tried to visit him at his home but he wasn't there.

FRIENDS

Weru . . . Weru . . . where are you?

STORYTELLER

Weru heard them calling. He tried to answer. But
when he tried to speak, he did not sound like
himself.

WERU

Here I am! Buck, buck, buck . . . Oh, no! I am
starting to sound like a chicken!

STORYTELLER

Poor Weru not only looked like a chicken now.
He sounded like one. He was so sad. He began
to cry.

FRIENDS

(Coming over to Weru's pen) Poor chicken. He
is sad.

STORYTELLER

Weru wanted to tell his friends who he was, but
all that came out of his mouth were chicken
sounds.

WERU

Buck, buck, buck . . .

STORYTELLER

The sorcerer came to visit Weru in his chicken pen.

SORCERER

Poor Weru. Are you tired of your disguise?

WERU

(Nodding his head) Buck . . . buck . . . buck.

SORCERER

I will take off your disguise then.

STORYTELLER

The sorcerer took off Weru's disguise. Weru was very happy.

WERU

Hooray! I am Weru again.

QUEEN

Look! Weru is in the chicken pen and my royal chicken is gone.

KING

Weru is better than a chicken. Come out of that pen, Weru.

WERU

I was the one who won the contest. I wanted to enter even though I had the chicken pox. So I made this chicken disguise.

QUEEN

You are a naughty boy, Weru.

KING

But he is also very clever.

SORCERER

Look, Weru, here come your friends.

(Weru's friends come on stage. They have pockmarks on their faces.)

FRIENDS

Weru! Weru! Look at us!

KING

Look! They have the chicken pox.

QUEEN

Now all of the children in the village have chicken pox. Can you cure them, Sorcerer?

SORCERER

Yes. We will have a pox picnic.

KING

What is a pox picnic?

SORCERER

You will see.

STORYTELLER

The sorcerer spread out a blanket.

(The Sorcerer spreads a blanket on the ground.)

SORCERER

Sit down, children.

(Weru and his friends sit in a circle on the blanket.)

STORYTELLER

Then the sorcerer got another big bag of peanuts and also a big bag of candy.

SORCERER

At a pox picnic, we have good things to eat. Here are candy and peanuts.

WERU AND HIS FRIENDS

(Eating the candy and peanuts) Yum! This is good.

KING

Is there any medicine you can give the children?

SORCERER

Yes. The best medicine. Laughter. You can help me.

(The Sorcerer gives the King and Queen each a feather; the Sorcerer had a feather also. They go around the circle tickling the children. The children laugh.)

SORCERER

Laugh louder, everyone. It will make you feel better.

(Weru and his friends laugh louder.)

STORYTELLER

Every day for ten days Weru and his friends had a pox party. They ate candy and peanuts and laughed. Soon they were well again and playing games.

(The children play a game where Weru holds a hula hoop and one at a time they hop through it.)

KING

Our children are all well again. I am happy.

QUEEN

But I am not. I still do not have a child. And now I do not even have my royal chicken.

WERU

Don't be sad. I will be your child.

QUEEN

You will, Weru? Thank you.

KING

Let him wear the crown. If he is your child, then he is the royal prince.

(The King puts the crown on Weru and everyone claps.)

STORYTELLER

So Weru became the queen's child and the prince of the village. And they all lived happily ever after.

(The Sorcerer tickles the King with a feather and the Queen, Weru, and his friends all laugh.)

STORYTELLER

The end.

(The actors take a bow.)

ABOUT THE AUTHOR

SHARON DENNIS WYETH has written a number of books for young readers, including *The Dinosaur Tooth* and *The Ghost Show* for the Annie K.'s Theater series, as well as the Pen Pals series. She is also a playwright and has written scripts for television. She lives with her husband and daughter in New York City.

ABOUT THE ILLUSTRATOR

HEIDI PETACH lives in Cincinnati, Ohio, with her husband and son. She has written and/or illustrated more than two dozen books for young readers, including *The Dinosaur Tooth* and *The Ghost Show* for the Annie K.'s Theater series.

SKYLARK BOOKS
can be *your* special friends

☐ 15615 **THE WHITE STALLION** by Elizabeth Shub.
$2.75 ($3.25 in Canada) Long ago, a proud white
stallion roamed the plains of Texas. Cowboys said
he was the greatest horse that ever lived. Gretchen
discovers, in a scary, exciting adventure, that they
were right.

☐ 15777 **JACK GALAXY, SPACE COP**
by Robert Kraus. $2.75 ($3.25 in Canada)
Jack zooms through the universe fighting space
crime with his best friend Sally and Jojo the space
dog. Giant hamburgers are taking over the world
and only Jack & his friends can save the day!

☐ 15711 **BUMPS IN THE NIGHT** by Harry Allard.
$2.50 ($2.95 in Canada) Dudley the Stork finds out
his new house is haunted and is determined to find
out just who the ghost is.

Buy them wherever paperback books are sold—or order below.
— — — — — — — — — — — — — — — — — — —

Bantam Books, Dept. SK12, 414 East Golf Road, Des Plaines, IL 60016

Please send me the items I have checked above. I am enclosing $_____
(please add $2.00 to cover postage and handling). Send check or money
order, no cash or C.O.D.s please.

Mr/Ms _____

Address _____

City/State _____ Zip _____

SK12-11/90

Please allow four to six weeks for delivery.
Prices and availability subject to change without notice.

Magical Skylark Adventures!

☐ **THE CASTLE IN THE ATTIC**
by Elizabeth Winthrop   15601 $3.50
William is sure there's something magical about the castle he receives
as a present. When he picks up the tiny silver knight, it comes to life!
Suddenly William is off on a fantastic quest to another land and time—
where a fiery dragon and an evil wizard are waiting to do battle...

☐ **THE PICOLINIS**
by Anne Graham Estern   15566 $2.75
Jessica and Peter Blake are thrilled when their parents buy a wonderful
antique dollhouse. But now they hear noises at night...music and voices
that seem to come from the dollhouse. Are the Picolini dolls alive?
The Blake children embark on an exciting and dangerous adventure
in search of lost treasure.

☐ **THE PICOLINIS AND THE HAUNTED HOUSE**
by Anne Graham Estern   15771 $2.95
Jessica and Peter discover a secret passageway in the house across the street
that thieves have been using for years. Now they want to find the thieves!
Can the Picolini dolls help them?

☐ **THE GHOST WORE GRAY**
by Bruce Coville   15610-1 $2.75
Sixth grader Nina Tanleven and her best friend Chris are visiting
an old country inn when suddenly the ghost of a young confederate soldier
appears! They know he's trying to tell them something. But what?

☐ **THE GHOST IN THE THIRD ROW**
by Bruce Coville   15646-2 $2.95
For Nina Tanleven nothing is scarier than trying out for a part in the school
play...except seeing a ghost sitting in the audience! Soon strange things
begin to happen and it's up to Nina to solve the mystery!

Buy them at your local bookstore or use this handy coupon for ordering:

Bantam Books, Dept. SK40, 414 East Golf Road, Des Plaines, IL 60016

Please send me the items I have checked above. I am enclosing $_____
(please add $2.00 to cover postage and handling). Send check or money
order, no cash or C.O.D.s please.

Mr/Ms _____

Address _____

City/State _____ Zip _____

SK40-12/90

Please allow four to six weeks for delivery.
Prices and availability subject to change without notice.

T · H · E
SADDLE CLUB

A blue-ribbon series by Bonnie Bryant

Stevie, Carole and Lisa are all very different, but they *love* horses! The three girls are best friends at Pine Hollow Stables, where they ride and care for all kinds of horses. Come to Pine Hollow and get ready for all the fun and adventure that comes with being 13!